THE BACCHAE

OF

EURIPIDES

translated by

Margaret Behr and Robert Banks Foster

Cover Image by Gellinger @ pixabay.com

First Edition

ISBN 978-0-9951941-8-2

EVA NOVA PRESS
PO Box 313
Kaslo, BC V0G 1M0

Dedicated to:

the memory of Professor Peter Smith

and

The Classics Department of the University of Victoria

What wisdom

should guide us?

What gift of the gods do people prize more

than a strong hand 880

to hold over an enemy's head?

Honour

is always

loved.

INTRODUCTION

"Can a sane man translate Euripides?" Shaw, Major Barbara.

EURIPIDES

In 408 B.C., Euripides, the last great ancient Greek dramatist, left Athens, over 70 and probably a broken man. An unsuccessful playwright laughed at by the comic poets, he fled the enemies he made with his criticisms of the city's politics and disastrous twenty year war with Sparta. After his death in exile in Macedonia in the winter of 408-06 B.C., *The Bacchae* was found among his papers. His son's production of it won first prize at the festival of Dionysus in Athens in 405.

DIONYSUS

Dionysus was the Greek god of wine. The fertility and the ecstasy associated with wine growing and drinking was celebrated in his name at seasonal festivals, which in Athens in the fifth century B.C. included the great spring drama festival. In *The Bacchae*, although Dionysus presents himself as a god who has in himself all the elements of a fully vital life, Euripides describes him as an insane god whose elements are at war with each other like the forces in the society around him.

In *The Bacchae,* Dionysus is at the same time the god of ecstasy, peace, and violence. Because of the festivals, the Athenians saw him as the god of theatre as well. Yet instead of offering us some kind of definitive statement in the name of the

5

festival's god, Euripides' character is unsure of his own authority.

We can infer that the claim of the festival to provide some divine truths is being questioned. Dionysus is especially unreliable in that he cannot be trusted with his mortal temper. The pronouncements he makes and that his followers make prove to be a destructive guide to finding a satisfying way to live. All he really has is power. By showing this god as seriously flawed, Euripides questions the values Dionysus represents and the religious authenticity of the festivals.

PLOT

Dionysus returns to his birth place in Greece after establishing his cult in the barbarian world of Asia Minor and Mesopotamia. Here in Thebes, Zeus had a brief love affair with Semele, a daughter of Cadmus, head of the city's ruling family. She became pregnant with Dionysus. Hera, Zeus' wife, in response to yet another of Zeus' infidelities, had Semele killed by a lightning bolt. But Zeus rescued the premature god, who was born a second time (with divine anatomical liberty) from Zeus' thigh. Accompanied by Asian Bacchantes, women followers who function as the chorus of the play, Dionysus has come back to revenge the slandering of his mother and the neglect of his cult.

Cadmus and Teiresias, the blind seer who in this play is a pedantic servant of many cults, agree that it is best for Thebes to at least pretend to worship this new god — there are, after all, some advantages to having a deity in the family. But Pentheus, Cadmus' grandson, the young ruler of Thebes to whom Cadmus has given up his power, rejects Dionysus on the grounds that women have authority and power in Dionysus' cult and that Dionysus forces them to be unchaste.

Dionysus gradually plays upon Pentheus' secret fascination with the women he scorns, making him lay down his arms and dress as a woman in order to spy on them in the mountains. There, driven mad by Dionysus, his mother, Agave, and her sisters tear him to pieces, returning to Thebes believing they have killed a lion. Seeing that their own actions brought about their downfall, the ruling family recognizes the full power of Dionysus' revenge; now they cannot avoid being forced into exile by the god.

THE CHORUS

Most scholars agree that the choral ode was the precursor of Athenian drama. Hymns to the gods and songs telling stories about the relationship between the gods and human beings were sung at the seasonal festivals. The first step in the development of Athenian drama occurred when an early dramatist had the choral leader step out to speak on his own and to interact with the chorus. Later dramatists like Aeschylus and Sophocles introduced two characters speaking with each other. It was probably Euripides' innovation that up to three characters speak together on stage at one time.

The role of the chorus changed in this process, usually becoming voices of the community that passively witnessed the action. In *The Bacchae*, the chorus' role has changed again. They are outsiders—the trusted worshippers of the god, caught upon the god's viewpoint. By the end of the play, they are followers caught in the paradox of being servants of an untrustworthy deity. They no longer merely celebrate the myth.

TRANSLATING AND INTERPRETATION

Translation involves interpretation and craft. To bring a work into our own time and language, writers have to lay the experience of the world they live in against their best understanding of the world that produced the original. Then they have to find language that bridges not only two tongues but two cultures.

With *The Bacchae,* we have attempted to make a translation that, while under no obligation to be literal to the text, sticks as close to it as our sense of language and theatre will allow. It is not a version or primarily an expression of our own ideas but our expression of our sense of Euripides. The stair step lines of the text are a verse form; the line numbers correspond to the Greek text.

We are especially grateful to Julian Reid for his precise suggestions on the original version and to Carl Hare, who directed a brilliant production of our translation.

Margaret Behr and Robert Banks Foster

NAMES OF THE ACTORS

DIONYSUS: *Greek god of wine, grape cultivation, fertility, ritual madness, religious ecstasy, and theatre (aka Bacchus or Bromius); son of the god Zeus and Semele, the daughter of Cadmus*

CADMUS: *Head of the ruling family of Thebes*

TEIRESIAS: *a blind seer and advisor to Cadmus*

PENTHEUS: *Cadmus' grandson, now ruler of Thebes*

AGAVE: *Pentheus' mother, daughter of Cadmus*

AUTONOE and INO: *Agave's sisters*

BACCHANTES: *Followers of Dionysus, including Agave, Autonoe, and Ino*

CHORUS

MESSENGER

SOLDIER

Other Soldiers and Servants

Dionysus enters and addresses the audience.

DIONYSUS:

I,
the son of Zeus,
            son of Semele, Cadmus' daughter,
brought to the birthing bed by lightning—
I, Dionysus,
have journeyed like a man
in man's shape
            with human stature
to the earth of Thebes
to stand by these rivers—   5
            Dirce and Ismenus.

Here is my mother's tomb.
Here she was struck by lightning.
Here where the fires of Zeus still smolder,
the ruins of her house
teach of Hera's undying wrath.

I traveled from the golden fields
of Lydia and Phrygia,   10
through the sun burnt plateau of Persia,
by Bactrian walls and the winter land of Media,   15
suddenly down to the shores of Arabia and Asia,
to white towered cities blessed by the bitter sea
where I taught all Greeks and foreigners alike   20
my dances and rites,
that I, Dionysus,

might be a god made known
to all peoples.

In Greece I visited Thebes first,
in revenge, charming the women till they cried with joy,
hanging fawn skins on their warm bodies,
forcing the ivy thyrsus into their hands   25
because these sisters of my mother claimed
that, I, Dionysus,
               was not born of Zeus,
claimed that Semele
slept with some man
and Cadmus cleverly
blamed the god for his daughter's sin.
Therefore, these women claimed,   30
Zeus killed that girl.

I have forced them
to wear the trappings
of my secret rites.
Now all the women of Thebes   35
sit under pale green
silver-firs
               on roofless crags.
This city must feel the power
of my Bacchic revels,   40
and know that I, Dionysus,
uphold the good name of my mother, Semele.
I am the god, revealed now to mortals,
whom she bore
               to immortal Zeus.

Cadmus has given his crown and all his power
to another daughter's son, Pentheus, an atheist,
who neglects me in his prayers,
who willfully ignores my power.   45

I will prove to him
and all Thebans
              that by birth
I am
              a god.

Then I will leave to take my light to other people.   50
But if the angry Thebans make war
upon the Bacchae in the mountains,
I shall lead an army of Maenads against them.
To do all this,
I have given myself human shape.
But you whom I led from Tmolus,   55
the holy mountain of Lydia,
my women of Asia, my dancing revelers,
you whom I cherished throughout our wanderings,
take in your hands
the tambourines
              of Phrygia,
Mother Rhea's invention
              and my own.
Make them ring about the palace of Pentheus   60
so that all the people of Cadmus
will come
              to watch my victory.
But for now

I will go to dance
          with the Bacchae
in the glens
          of Cithaeron.

Exit Dionysus as the chorus enters.

CHORUS:

From Asia,   65
from sacred Tmolus,
I run to Bromius,
whose service is sweet and easy.
Come cry *Evohe* to Bacchus!

You there and you there and you,
in the streets, in the houses,
make way for our dancing,   70
keep silent and pure,
as I sing
of the rites
          of Holy Dionysus.

Strophe

Blest is the one
whom the gods have taught their mysteries;
who, pious and chaste, finds joy in the hills at the festivals
of Bacchus;   75
who, hallowed and pure through Cybele's rites,
praises the great mother,
shakes the thyrsus,

is crowned with ivy,   80
and honours
Dionysus.

Bacchae, Bacchae,
bear Dionysus home,
bear Bromius, God's son,   85
from the fields of Phrygia

to Greece
where the streets
are wide for dancing.

Antistrophe

He was born too early.
He was born in pain.
He was forced from the womb
of his dead mother.   90
He was hidden by Zeus
deep in Zeus' thigh,
and the flesh was bound   95
with brooches of gold
to hide him from the eyes of Hera.
He was born a second time,
a young god, bull-horned.   100
Zeus crowned him with serpents;
and Maenads now,
remembering,
wind round their braids
garlands of thin snakes.

14

Strophe

Thebes,
City of Semele,   105
grow green.
Wind in wool
branches of oak and fir.
Crown yourself   110
with ivy,
with red-berried bryony.

In a fawn skin, dance
and be reverent
bearing your violent staves.

For Bromius   115
leads us wide-eyed through the land,
to the mountains
where women stray from their looms,
stung to madness
by holy Dionysus.

Antistrophe

Praise
the Curetes caves,   120
the sacred dens of Crete where Zeus was born.
There the Corybantes   125
made me a drum
to mingle with the flutes' sighing,
and gave this to mother Rhea
in their revels

to accompany her women's cries,
but wine-mad satyrs   130
stole it
and took it to humans
so
each second spring
we dance to its beat
to delight
our holy
Dionysus.

Epode

Ready to hunt
we please the god,   135
we
who fall to the earth in ecstasy,
we
who delight in filling our mouths with live flesh
and drinking the blood of slaughtered goats,
we shout
from the mountains of Lydia and Phrygia,   140
Evohe
to Bromius
who leads where the earth
flows with milk,
flows with wine,
flows with honey,
where the rioter's pine torch   145
trails smoke
sweet as Syrian frankincense

behind him
as he runs!

Our hair   150
tosses
        in the wind.
We shout
while Bromius roars,
"Bacchae! Bacchae!
Pride of golden Tmolus,
        praise Evius, Lord of joy,   155
with Phrygian cries,
with tambourine beats,
with the sweet sound of flutes!   160

Run joyful
in the mountains!
Roam wild
in the mountains!"   165
And we
like young colts
with their grazing mothers,
we Bacchantes,
with feet that fly,
dance!

Enter Teiresias and later Cadmus dressed as Bacchantes
except that their costumes are very untidy.

TEIRESIAS:

Who's at the gates? 170
Call Cadmus from the house—
Cadmus, Agenor's son,
who came from Sidon
      and built the towers
      that defend this city of Thebes.
Go tell Cadmus
that Teiresias
is looking for him.
      He knows
why I'm here,
an old man 175
      come to fetch
an older man
to wear a fawn skin,
      to make a thyrsus,
crowning our sticks and heads with wreaths of ivy.

Enter Cadmus.

CADMUS:

My dear friend
is that your voice?
I thought I heard
      words of wisdom
spoken at my door.
I'm quite ready,
dressed precisely 180
as the god commands.

18

We must dress up for him
since he is the son of my daughter . . .

    since
Dionysus
is most certainly

    a god . . .

      In any case,
we must
magnify his greatness

    with our praise.
Now, where shall we dance?

    Where shall we stamp our feet
    and shake our gray heads?   185
Tell me, old man to old man, Teiresias—
you're wise—explain
why I won't get tired
dancing night and day,
striking the earth with my thyrsus.
This joy we feel makes us forget
that we're old men.

TEIRESIAS:

Exactly.
I'm young again   190
and ready to dance!

CADMUS:

We shall drive our chariot
to the mountains . . .

TEIRESIAS:

Riding in luxury
is no way to honour a god.

CADMUS:

Must I worry about your health
even in my old age?

TEIRESIAS:

Listen,
the god won't let us get tired
when he leads the way.

CADMUS:

Are we the only men in the city   195
who dance for Bacchus?

TEIRESIAS:

Of course; no one else has enough sense.

CADMUS:

Well then,
I see no need to linger here.
                    Give me your hand.

TEIRESIAS:

There it is.

CADMUS:

At least I am one man who doesn't despise the gods.

TEIRESIAS:

No, we   200
don't engage
        in clever arguments
           about divinity;
our father's customs, ancient as time,
are good enough for us,
and, certainly,
no vain words
        from these bright young men
are going to change our minds.
Of course,
some will say
        that I dishonour old age
in dancing,
ivy-crowned,
        but that's not true.   205
The god rejects
neither child nor
        elder
who feels inspired
to dance.
He wishes honour
from everyone.
He wants all,
from high to low,

to glorify
him.

CADMUS:

Teiresias,
since the light of day
is the one light you can't see,
I must explain to you
what's happening.
Here comes my grandson, Pentheus,
toward the palace.
He's king now, remember.
He's almost running.
He looks very upset.
I wonder what
troubles him.

Enter Pentheus.

PENTHEUS:

While I was away,
I heard rumours
of corruption in Thebes.
How our women
had run off
to celebrate
perverse rites
in the mountains,
roaming about with this
brand new god, Dionysus—

210

215

22

whoever he is.

Everywhere,
       in the midst of their revels
              stand full wine bowls.   220

And women slink off
one by one
to copulate
with any man
       who happens by.

They pretend to be Maenads, priestesses.

It's Aphrodite,   225
not Bacchus,
       they worship.

I caught as many as I could.

My servants
keep them safe
       in prison.

As for the rest,
I will hunt them out of the mountains,
       as they deserve:

even members
of my own family—

Agave, my mother,
who once bore me to Echion, her sister,
       Ino,
and even Autone, the mother of Acteon,
my dead cousin.   230

I'll put an end
to these disgusting rites.

They say

that some friendly stranger
                has come,
a cheat from Lydia
who howls out enchantments,
a man with
sweet, golden   235
                locks of hair,
with "wine-dark" eyes
and the "grace
                of Aphrodite,"
a man
who consorts
                day and night
                        with young girls,
dangling all sorts of
"Bacchic mysteries"
                before their eyes.
If I
can capture him
I shall break   240
his ringing thyrsus,
cut
his waving hair,
sever his head from his body.
This man
says Dionysus is a god,
                once sewn in Zeus' thigh.
A thunderbolt
burnt Dionysus to ashes
when his mother lied   245

that Zeus

        had loved her.
This stranger deserves
torture and death

        for his outrageous lies.
What!
Well, here's another marvel!
The seer Teiresias
in a dappled fawn skin,
and my grandfather too!
How ludicrous   250
the bacchic wand looks
in your hands!
I cannot bear the sight
of old men

        who have lost their senses!
Throw away that ivy
and that

        thyrsus!
Teiresias,
let my grandfather's hand go!

        You misled him.   255
You wanted all this,
to foist this new god on men

        and then collect
still more gold
for your fake auguries
and vile burnt offerings.
If I didn't respect your old age,
I'd chain you

with the Bacchae
for introducing these 260
filthy rituals.
There is no good in these festivals
where shimmering wine
corrupts women.

CHORUS:

You dishonour
our gods,
son of Echion.
You shame your house, Cadmus,
and all his mortal children!

TEIRESIAS:

Wisdom from the wise
surprises no one.
But your clever tongue
makes you seem wise
when you have no understanding.
Rash eloquence 270
is society's disaster.
One person speaks in ignorance
and leads thousands astray.
Now, no one knows what strength,
what greatness this new god at whom you jeer
will have in Greece.
But let me tell you
there are two powers over us,
sometimes called "the dry" and "the wet."

The first is personified by the goddess Demeter   275
or Earth—whichever you wish to call her;
she nourishes mortals with dry food,
with bread.
This new god, Semele's child,
has come with a matching gift,
a crystalline liquid
from clustered grapes
which he generously brought to end
          all human suffering.   280
Wine
fills the emptiness
          in the grieved heart
and helps us forget
in blissful sleep.
His is the only medicine
to cure our pain.
And remember this,
when we pour libations
          to the gods,   285
it is wine, Dionysus' gift,
that sends our prayers to heaven.
So, through him
come all good things.
But you—
you laugh at Dionysus,
just because people say
he once was sewn in Zeus' thigh.
I shall explain what really happened.
Zeus snatched the baby from the thunderbolt's fire

and carried him to Olympus.
But Hera wished Dionysus   290
cast from heaven,
so Zeus cunningly
molded a child
            from a fragment of sky
and gave this to Hera
as hostage
            for his future good behaviour.

Later they quarreled
over this dummy,
and people who lived
in that part of the country,
when they passed the story
from door to door,
confused this word for "hostage"
with their word for "thigh" and thought
that Dionysus
            had been sewn in Zeus' thigh.   295
That should make it perfectly clear
how the story began.
Moreover,
Dionysus
is a god
            of prophecy,
for in the Bacchanalian revels
and the Bacchanalian ecstasy
when the god enters   300
the worshiper's body
            the future

is revealed.
Sometimes, too,
he assumes the functions of Aries;
            when panic strikes an army
before a spear has been thrown,
this madness
descends from Dionysus.   305
Soon you shall see him
on the crags
            above Delphi,
leaping in the heights of Parnassus
with pine torches
or green branches
            in his hands.
Soon he will be
a great god
            throughout Greece.
Pentheus,
let me persuade you.
            No one can change fate.
Do not mistake your fantasies   310
for wisdom.
Welcome the god
to our country,
pour him
a libation,
dance,
crown your head
            with ivy.
It is true

that Dionysus does not
            force chastity
            on women in love,   315
but those who are chaste by nature
are not seduced
during his Bacchic rites.
When a crowd meets you at the gates
and the city   320
glorifies the name of Pentheus,
            you rejoice.
Dionysus also
enjoys honour—
and deserves it.
Therefore,
we crown ourselves with ivy.
            Though you laugh at Cadmus and me,
we old men
must dance.
We must not   325
be swayed by your words
            to rebel against a god.
Your mind is diseased.
No drug can cure you.

CHORUS:

Even Apollo would approve your logic—
your praise of Dionysus.

CADMUS: 330

Young man,
Teiresias has given you
　　　　　some very good advice.
Do as we do,
don't rebel;
for the moment

run along
and stop trying to be wise.
Even if the god—
as you say,
　　　　　is not a god,
for the moment
accept him.
Then Semele   335
will be thought
　　　　　the mother of a god
and everyone
will honour
　　　　　our family.
Besides,
remember what happened
　　　　　to Acteon,
how the wild hounds
he had raised
tore him to pieces
in the mountain glades
when he boasted
he
　　　　　was a mightier hunter
　　　　　　　　than Artemis.   340

To protect you
I will crown you with ivy.
Come with us
and honour the god.

PENTHEUS:

Keep your hands off me, Bacchant!
Don't infect me
with your madness!
As for this man who drove you insane,   345
send a soldier
to the throne
           on which Teiresias sits
               when he prophesies.
Order him to break this seat to pieces
and scatter the "holy flowers"
           to wind and storm.   350
And this effeminate stranger
who brought this new sickness to women,
keeping them
from their husband's beds,
drag him here   355
in chains.
          We will stone him to death.
He shall bitterly regret
coming to Thebes.

Exit Pentheus.

32

TEIRESIAS:

You foolish child,
you don't understand the consequences
        of anything you say!
You're not just stupid,
you're insane!
Cadmus,
let us go
        and pray for this man,
though he acts like a barbarian.
We must
gain pardon   360
        for Thebes,
so that no god's vengeance
strike our city.
Come with me.
We'll help each other along.
It would be shameful for us to fall.   365
Come what may,
we must serve Bacchus.
Cadmus, beware.
Pentheus' name means "sorrow."
He may bring sadness to your house.
I need no skill in prophecy to know
that the tongue of a fool
        makes a foolish noise.

Exit Teiresias and Cadmus.

CHORUS:

Strophe

Holiness, queen of the gods,
stretching your golden wings across the earth,   370
do you hear the word of Pentheus?
Do you hear this blasphemy
against Bromius   375
whom reason and joy together
have crowned foremost of the gods?
He leads us
with dances, with laughter,   380
making care disappear in the grape's fire, in feasting,
before he casts sleep from the wine-bowls
on ivy-wreathed revelers.   385

Antistrophe

To those whose mouths spout folly
quick destruction comes.
But those who live quietly
in wisdom—
their houses last.
Freed from the world,
they see mortals
from the purer air of heaven.
Cleverness   390
is not wisdom,
and those who'd seem wise as the gods—
their lives will be short.
Those who seek greatness

will not see the snake at their feet.
Mad ways   400
set all on the road to disaster.

Strophe

I long for Aphrodite's island,
Cyprus and the city of Paphos
where Love lives freely
and delights mortal beings.
I long to walk by the hundred-mouthed Nile
who makes green a land that never feels rain.
I long to see the home of the Muses,
Pieria, on the slopes of Olympus.   410
Bromius! Bromius! Evius! God!
Lead me there,
for there the Graces,
there Love,
there all are free to honour Dionysus.   415

Antistrophe

This god, the child of Zeus,
loves feasting
loves joy brought
by the nursemaid goddess, Peace.   420
To the blessed rich
and to the poor
he brings wine that eases pain.
But those
who refuse
to live blessed by happiness   425

he hates.
Be wise!
Shun humans
who meddle with the gods.
The ways of common people I accept.   430

Enter several soldiers with Dionysus in chains.

Enter Pentheus.

SOLDIER:

Pentheus!
We have captured the prey
for which you sent us,   435
        but the man you called "beast"
           proved tame;
he made no attempt to escape,
but even helped us bind his hands.
He didn't turn pale
but instead smiled
and ordered us   440
to obey you.
I was ashamed of my duty
and told him
that I didn't wish to bind him,
that I was just leading him to you
at your command.
And I have other news—
the Bacchantes
whom you imprisoned   445
have escaped to the meadow-lands

where they dance and praise Bromius.
The chains fell from their feet
and the bars of their cells were withdrawn
                    as if by magic.
This man who has come to Thebes
seems full of power.
I'm glad he's   450
your responsibility
                    now.

PENTHEUS:

Unbind his hands.
Now we've caught him,
he won't be quick enough
                    to escape me.
I see why the women
you desire
                    find you attractive.
Your body would suit them.
Your long hair
flows suggestively
                    over your cheek—
you're no wrestler!   455
And that pale skin
comes from sleeping all day
to gain strength
for the nightly rites of Aphrodite.
Now,   460
what's your nationality?

DIONYSUS:

Easily told.
You've heard of the river Tmolus
with its fields of flowers.

PENTHEUS:

Yes, it rings the city of Sardis.

DIONYSUS:

I come from there. Lydia is my country.

PENTHEUS:

What made you bring your rites to Greece?   465

DIONYSUS:

Dionysus, the son of Zeus, initiated us.

PENTHEUS:

I take it that in Lydia you have a different Zeus
who begets new gods.

DIONYSUS:

No, we worship the same Zeus
who married Semele here in Thebes.

PENTHEUS:

Did he really compel you to come here?
Were you awake or did you dream it all?

DIONYSUS:

He told me his secret rites   470
face to face.

PENTHEUS:

And what are these rites of yours?

DIONYSUS:

The uninitiate must not be told!

PENTHEUS:

How do they benefit the initiate?

DIONYSUS:

You've no right to know;
yet you'd find them
                          well worth knowing.

PENTHEUS

You have a cunning way   475
of making me more curious.

DIONYSUS:

We who worship the god
hate the impious.

PENTHEUS:

You saw the god clearly?
What was he like?

DIONYSUS:

He could take whatever form he wished.

PENTHEUS:

Clever words again, but they say nothing.

DIONYSUS:

Only a fool
takes a warning
           as an insult.

480

PENTHEUS:

Did you come here first to introduce the god?

DIONYSUS:

No. In every other land
they celebrate these mysteries.

PENTHEUS:

It's clear they're not as wise as the Greeks.

DIONYSUS:

No, they're wiser, even though their customs are strange.

PENTHEUS:

Do you perform your rituals by day or night?   485

DIONYSUS:

By night. We believe that darkness is holy.

PENTHEUS:

It's a cunning time to force filth upon women.

DIONYSUS:

Vice thrives in daylight too.

PENTHEUS:

You shall suffer for all your cunning evasions.

DIONYSUS:

And you for your blasphemy and stupidity.   490

PENTHEUS:

How clever the Bacchant is with words!

DIONYSUS:

What dire punishment will you make me suffer?

PENTHEUS:

First, I shall cut off
your pretty love-locks.

DIONYSUS:

My hair is sacred.
I grew it for the god.

PENTHEUS:

Next,   495
I shall take your thyrsus
            from your hands.

DIONYSUS:

Go ahead, take it,
but remember
            it belongs to Dionysus.

PENTHEUS:

We will imprison you
for now.

DIONYSUS:

Whenever I wish,
the god himself
            will free me.

PENTHEUS:

No doubt—
when you are seated in chains
            with the other Bacchantes!

DIONYSUS:

He is here now   500
and sees what I suffer.

PENTHEUS:

Where? I can't see him.

DIONYSUS:

He is wherever I am.
You, being unholy, cannot see him.

PENTHEUS:

Take this man away. He mocks both me
                    and Thebes.

DIONYSUS:

I forbid you to chain me!
But I speak wisdom among fools.

PENTHEUS:

We shall bind you; I rule here.   505

DIONYSUS:

You do not know who you are
or what you do.

PENTHEUS:

I am Pentheus,
son of Agave,
            son of Echion.

DIONYSUS:

That your name means "sorrow"
is highly appropriate.

PENTHEUS:

Take him away.
Lock him up in darkness,   510
so he can dance with his women.
We shall enslave them,
silence their beating drums,
and put them to work behind my looms.

DIONYSUS:

I shall go now   515
but I shall not suffer.
Dionysus (who you say does not exist)
will demand retribution
on behalf of this man
you unjustly lead away
            in chains.

Exit Dionysus, Pentheus, and the soldiers.

CHORUS:

Strophe

Achelous' daughter,
queen and blessed maiden,
flowing river of Dirce   520
who held Bromius safe from the fire
before Zeus caught him up and named him,   525
before Zeus proclaimed
that Thebes one day would honour
twice-born Dithyrambus.
Blessed Dirce, why   530
do you banish me
who brought my dances to your banks?
Why do you flee my ivy crown?
Soon you will know the blessed power of wine.   535
Soon you will heed Bacchus.

Antistophe

Pentheus' deeds prove
his house sprang from dirt—
Echion grew from a dragon's tooth   540
sown in the earth by Cadmus.
That monster must have giant's blood
to fight the generous gods,
to catch us in his nets and bind us,   545
to chain my fellow dancers
in the darkness of his house.
Do you see this,   550
son of Zeus?

Do you see your servants oppressed?
Come to us
with your golden thyrsus!
Descend from Olympus!
Destroy this man!   555

Epode

Dionysus,
is it Nysa
where wild beasts feed or the peaks of Corcyia?
In what land
are you king?
Is it the glades of Olympus   560
where Orpheus
with his harp
gathered the trees with his music,
herded beasts in the wilderness with his song?
Is it Pieria,   565
where Evius
in choral dance and festival,
whirls with the Maenads   570
over the tumbling Axius
over Lydias' torrent?
Will we find him there
in that land
whose horses are famous,
where waters
enrich the Earth
bringing wealth   575
to humans?

DIONYSUS:

Off stage

Bacchae, hear
my
cry!

CHORUS:

Who
shouts?
Who calls
me?

DIONYSUS:

I, Dionysus,   580
son of Semele,
son of Zeus.

CHORUS:

Come
to your
revelers,
Lord.

DIONYSUS:

Queen   585
of the
Earthquake,
shake

the ground
>   of Thebes!

CHORUS:

Make the house of Pentheus shake!
Make the house of Pentheus crumble!   590
Make the house of Pentheus fall!

Praise Dionysus.
Let all honour him!

See how the pillars shake!
See how the beams shatter!

Hear Bromius roar
within the house!

DIONYSUS:

Torches of thunder,   595
consume the house of Pentheus!

CHORUS:

I see
the fire of Zeus
>   round the holy tomb of Semele.

Tremble on the ground
for Bacchus has come

and thrown the houses down!   600
Worship the child of Zeus!

Enter Dionysus.

DIONYSUS:

My women of Asia,
are you so panic-stricken
            that you tremble on the ground?
Since it seems that Dionysus   605
has destroyed the house of Pentheus,
            stand up and rejoice!
There's no need to be afraid.

CHORUS:

O god who shines on our revels,
how happy I am to find you.
I was lost
and alone.

DIONYSUS:

What? Did your hearts sink   610
when Pentheus threw me
            into his dark prison?

CHORUS:

How could I help
being afraid?

Who would protect me
if you were gone?

How were you freed
from that man's power?

DIONYSUS:

I humiliated him,
confused his mind

        so he didn't touch me,
but when he found a bull 615
inside the stalls
he led the beast to prison
and hurled chains around
        its legs and hooves.

I sat nearby
and watched him pant with rage.
He bit his lips
as sweat streamed off his body. 620

Then Bacchus shook the house,
and lit a fire on his mother's tomb.
Pentheus, of course, thought his own house was on fire,
and ran everywhere,
ordering his slaves to fetch water— 625

rather pointless I thought.
Suddenly,
afraid that I might escape,
he snatched up his sword and rushed inside.

Then Bromius created
an image of himself in the courtyard.

50

Pentheus ran in 630
and started stabbing the breeze
          trying to slaughter me.

Then Bacchus
humiliated him
          still more.
Pentheus' house
was shattered
          as reward for my imprisonment.
Now he is exhausted;
he has thrown his sword away;
a man
who dared fight a god. 635

In the meantime, I strolled here
without a thought for Pentheus.
But now I hear his footsteps;
I wonder what he will say.
I will endure his fury easily. 640
The wise man has a reasonable temper.

Enter Pentheus.

PENTHEUS:

I have been tricked, tortured!
The stranger I chained escaped.
Now he is here. 645
How could you escape from my house?

DIONYSUS:

Calm yourself.
Be still.
               Put a quiet foot
                         under your anger.

PENTHEUS:

How did you escape from my prison?

DIONYSUS:

I told you that someone would set me free.

PENTHEUS:

Who?   650
I can't understand your nonsense.

DIONYSUS:

The god who brought wine to man.

PENTHEUS:

A vile god.

DIONYSUS:

[Be careful,
he is near enough
               to hear you.
Though you don't believe in Dionysus,
he is now

52

in all his power
within this city.]

PENTHEUS:

Soldiers,
bar the gates to the women's quarters!

DIONYSUS:

Do you think gods
can't step over walls?

PENTHEUS:

Very clever,
but show more sense.

DIONYSUS:

I'll show my wisdom   655
when it is needed.

Enter Messenger

But now,
listen to this man's story,
he brings you news
from the mountains.
I promise
we won't run away.

MESSENGER:

I have fled from great Mount Cithaeron 660
where the drifting white snow

> never, day or night,
> summer or winter,

ceases its downward
downward   falling . . .

PENTHEUS:

Get to the point.

MESSENGER:

I have seen the Bacchae,
the wild women 665

> who darted barefoot
> from this city.

I would like to tell
you and your people

> about the miracles they do.

May I speak freely—
without fear of offending
your royal temper? 670

PENTHEUS:

Whatever your tale,
tell it.

> No one should be angered
> when he hears the truth.

Besides,

the more terrible the things
                you tell us,
the greater will be the punishment
                we inflict on this man
who teaches our women such rites.   675

MESSENGER:

At daybreak,
just as the cattle were moving
into the highest part of the meadow-lands
and the sun began to warm the earth,
I saw them: 680
three bands of women—
one led by Autonoe,
the second by Agave,
                your mother,
and the third by Ino.

All were sleeping, exhausted—
some on boughs of silver fir,
some on beds of oak leaves—   685
resting, quite chastely, on the ground.
Not one,
as you described,
drunk on wine and the flutes' sighing.

Not one
hunting alone through the woods for love.

Suddenly,
your mother woke.

She heard the lowing
        of our horned cattle,
and standing up

cried aloud
to rouse the other Bacchae.   690

One
      by
            one

they rose,
like slow-moving birds,
ordered,
        calm,
shaking sleep
from their eyes—
old and young,
wives
and
        unmarried girls.

First they unbound their hair   695
and let it fall loose
        on their shoulders.

Then they tightened
the clasps on their fawn skins,
        and around their heads
wound snakes
        with flickering tongues.

Some,
who had left
                    new-born children
                            at home,
cradled
large-eyed fawns
                    and wolf cubs
                            in their arms,

gently giving   700
white milk
                    from their still-swollen
                            breasts.
They crowned themselves
with wreaths
                    of ivy, oak, and bryony.

One
struck a rock
                    with her thyrsus—
clear water tumbled out.   705
Another
plunged her staff
                    into the ground
and fountains of wine   710
flowed from the earth.

Others still
scratched at the soil and found milk
or from their thyrsi
drank drops of honey.

If you had been there,
even you

            would have honoured

the god
you now condemn.

While we herdsmen argued   715
about the marvels,
someone with a clever tongue
who had wandered up from the city
began to confuse us—calling us "gentlemen"—
suggesting
that to earn your thanks,
we should chase your mother Agave   720
away from the other revelers.
Somehow
this seemed

             to make sense,

so we hid in the bushes
and waited to ambush the Bacchae.

Suddenly
all of them,
at the same instant,
waved their thyrsi
and shouted with one voice
to Bacchus, son of Zeus.   725

Then the mountains
and the beasts of the mountains
were possessed by the god,

and as they moved
it seemed for a moment
the world moved with them.

Agave
ran near me;
I leaped out to catch her;   730
she cried to her Bacchantes as if they were hounds
and with their thyrsi
they hunted us.

We escaped
being torn to pieces
only because
they attacked our cattle instead of us.
The weakest of the Bacchantes   735
with her bare hands
tore the limbs
from a bellowing calf,
while more powerful women
cracked the bones
                of full-grown cows.
Severed hooves,   740
ribs,
                and red flesh
were strewn on the grass;
blood defiled
                even the silver firs.

Before this day
a bull's horns

were feared;
now bulls are drawn to the earth

by the hands of girls.
Bulls' hides   745
are stripped from their flesh
faster
than even a king's eye
                could see.

Like a huge flock of birds they descended
to the rich plains of Asopus,
                where our Theban grain grows ripe,   750
and swept on
down Cithaeron
through Hysinae and Erythrae,
like invaders pillaging homes
driving the people before them,
snatching up children
                with the rest of their plunder,
easily carrying it all
                poised on their shoulders.   755
No bronze, no iron could resist them.
Fire burned in their hair,
yet did not burn them.

Soon the angry villagers armed themselves
and then, O King, you would have seen   760
a marvel, for spears
drew no blood
                from the Bacchantes

or loosened the thyrsi
from their hands.
Instead,
women wounded men,
women forced men
to retreat.
Then the Bacchantes ran to the hills,   765
to the fountains
that the god created to purify their bodies,
while snakes round their braids
licked from their cheeks
drops of blood.

O King,
whoever this god may be,
welcome him
to our city
for he has many powers.   770
They say
he brought wine
to end our suffering,
and truly, without it
there is no love
nor any other pleasure
left.

CHORUS:

Though I fear to speak   775
before such a king,
I still proclaim

that Dionysus

        is a true god.

PENTHEUS:

This Bacchic insolence
blazes up like fire,
a disgrace to all Greeks!
We must march   780
now!
Order all shield-bearers, horsemen, and bowmen:
meet me at the Electran gates
to war on the Bacchae.
How can we stand   785
for such violence
from women!

DIONYSUS:

Nothing changes your mind,
though you hear my words,
though I speak for your own good
        while you make me suffer.
I repeat,
stay at peace.
Do not arm against the god.
Bromius   790
will not permit you to rage amid
his mountains.

PENTHEUS:

Stop preaching!
Do you want to remain free?

DIONYSUS:

Make the god an offering.
Don't struggle against his strength
like a sacrificial beast.   795

PENTHEUS:

His women shall be my sacrifices!
My strength shall be seen
in the glens
                    of Cithaeron.

DIONYSUS:

No,
you will flee,
your brazen shields
beaten into disgrace
by Bacchic thyrsi.

PENTHEUS:

It's pointless to wrestle with this stranger.
Chained or free, he keeps on talking.   800

DIONYSUS:

Lord Pentheus,
we can still
bring our quarrel
       to a satisfactory
         conclusion.

PENTHEUS:

Only if you become a slave
to my slaves.

DIONYSUS:

I shall lead the women here unarmed.

PENTHEUS

What trap   805
are you preparing
       for me?

DIONYSUS:

I only wish to save you.

PENTHEUS:

You've already pledged yourself to these women.

DIONYSUS:

I pledged myself—to the god.

PENTHEUS:

Stop talking nonsense.
Fetch my arms!

DIONYSUS:

Stop! 810
Calm yourself.
Listen.
Would you like to see
them huddled together
upon the mountains?

PENTHEUS:

To see their rites,
I'd give more gold than I could count.

DIONYSUS:

Why this sudden lust?

PENTHEUS:

Well, it would be upsetting
to see them drunk . . .

DIONYSUS:

But though upsetting, 815
it would give you pleasure?

PENTHEUS:

Yes.
We must hide behind the silver firs.

DIONYSUS:

If you hide,
they will pull you out.

PENTHEUS:

True. We dare not go secretly.

DIONYSUS:

I will lead you there.
Shall we go?

PENTHEUS:

Take me quickly.   820
I cannot wait. . .

DIONYSUS:

You must wear a fine linen dress.

PENTHEUS:

Why?
Must I be made
to look like a woman?

DIONYSUS:

They might kill a *man* who watched them.

PENTHEUS:

True again.
You seem to know what to do.

DIONYSUS:

Dionysus taught me   825
this music well.

PENTHEUS:

How will I get ready?

DIONYSUS:

I shall put a dress on you.

PENTHEUS:

A dress?
A woman's dress?
          How could I bear the shame?

DIONYSUS:

Then you no longer want
to watch the Maenads?

PENTHEUS:

You will put a dress on my body. 830

DIONYSUS:

And then a wig
of long yellow hair.

PENTHEUS:

And what else?

DIONYSUS:

A long robe, a band around your head . . .

PENTHEUS:

And then?

DIONYSUS:

A thyrsus in your hand 835
and a dappled fawn skin
round your body.

PENTHEUS:

Not as a woman!
I couldn't bear it!
I am a man
from a family ruled by men.

DIONYSUS:

Blood will flow
if you battle
        with the women.

PENTHEUS:

That also is true.
We must spy on them
        first.

DIONYSUS:

It is wise to hunt evil with evil.

PENTHEUS:

But how can I walk   840
through Thebes
        without being seen?

DIONYSUS:

Oh, we'll pick the empty streets—
I'll lead you.

PENTHEUS:

Well,
I shall go with you,   845
for either I take up arms
or accept your plan.

Pentheus exits.

DIONYSUS:

My women,
a man has fallen into our net—
to die at the hands of the Bacchae.

        Dionysus
        what will happen
        depends on you;
        I know you are near.

Let us make Pentheus pay—   850
drive him mad!
If he is not insane
        he will not put on
            a woman's dress.

But I want him
the laughing stock of Thebes
as I lead him like a woman through the streets.
I shall dress Pentheus   855
in the clothes he will wear to Hades,
slain by his mother's hands.
He shall learn
that Dionysus
        is the son of Zeus,
a god with the power of a god,   860
a god most fearful
and most gentle.

Exit Dionysus.

CHORUS:

Strophe

Shall I soon be free again to dance,
to toss my head all night   865
in the dew-filled air?
Like a fawn far
from the watchers,
the twisted nets,   870
the huntsmen urging on their hounds,
like a fawn playing
in the green joy of a meadow, far
from the storm-blown troubles of the world,
like a fawn leaping through green valleys to the forest,
shall I be free to dance   875
amid the gentle leaves?

What wisdom
should guide us?
What gift of the gods do people prize more
than a strong hand   880
to hold over an enemy's head?
Honour
is always
loved.

Antistrophe

Slowly they begin,
but always the powers of heaven punish
those fools who ignore the gods,   885

those fools who will not give praise
through wine-mad dreams.

For them the gods hunt,
stepping softly behind the curtains
awaiting
those who profane them.

Nothing is stronger
than ancient laws.   890
Learn them! Live by them!
With ease
use their power!
What the gods preserve   895
in the foundations
            of the world
these truths
endure
            forever.

What wisdom
should guide us?
What gift of the gods do people prize more
than a strong hand   900
to hold over
an enemy's head?
Honour
is always
loved.

Epode

Blessed is the one
who finds a harbour
safe from the winter sea.

Blessed is the one
who travels beyond affliction.
Blessed is the one   905
who wins great joy.
Numberless more
have their dreams.
Some hopes are fulfilled,
some vanish.

Whoever lives happily   910
from day to day
                    I bless.

Enter Dionysus.

DIONYSUS:

So,
you're eager to see
                    what must not be seen
and hunt
                    what should never be hunted.

Come out,
come out, Pentheus,
                    you mad woman, you Bacchante,   915
come out to spy

on your mother

        and her company.

Enter Pentheus.

Well, you
certainly look

        like one of Cadmus' daughters.

PENTHEUS:

I seem to see two suns in the sky, and two
cities of Thebes,
each with its seven gates,
and you
who lead me   920

        seem a bull!
Were you a beast
all this time?

DIONYSUS:

You see
clearly

        now.
The god hated you before
but now he helps

        guide us.

PENTHEUS:

How do I look?   925
Don't I carry myself just like Ino?

Am I not as poised
as my mother Agave?

DIONYSUS:

As I watch you
I imagine I see
                those women.
But isn't one of your curls out of place?
I thought I'd pinned it safely under your hair band.

PENTHEUS:

In the house   930
I was shaking
                with Bacchic frenzy;
it must have slipped out again.

DIONYSUS:

I'll be your maid
and rearrange it.
Tilt your head back a little.

*There should be something slightly horrifying about the way
Dionysus tilts Pentheus' head back, exposing Pentheus' throat.*

PENTHEUS:

Yes, take care of everything.
I depend on you now.

DIONYSUS:

Your girdle's not tied properly;   935
the pleats of your dress don't hang straight.

PENTHEUS:

On the right side it's down by my foot
but on the left, it's above my ankle.

DIONYSUS:

You will think me the best of friends
when I show you,   940
no matter what people say,
        the Bacchae
            are sober and chaste.

PENTHEUS:

In which hand
should I hold the thyrsus
        to look more like a Bacchant?

DIONYSUS:

In your right.
And strike the ground
        when you stamp your right foot.
How glad I am
that your mind
        has been
           changed.

PENTHEUS:

Do you think I can bear the weight   945
of Cithaeron and
its Bacchae
                    on my shoulders?

DIONYSUS:

If you wish.
Now you begin to understand.
                    Before you were not sane.

PENTHEUS:

Should we take levers   950
or should I tear it up with my hands?

DIONYSUS:

Surely you don't want to destroy
the nymphs' shrines
and the sanctuaries
"where sound the pipes of Pan"!

PENTHEUS:

Quite right.
We must not conquer these women by force.
I'll hide in the silver firs.

DIONYSUS:

You will hide
and be hidden as befits a man
            who spies on Maenads.

PENTHEUS:

I can see them now,
like mating birds
            embracing in the bushes!

DIONYSUS:

That is exactly
how you will surprise them,
if they don't surprise you first.

PENTHEUS:

Escort me through the principal streets of Thebes!
Let all the men know
only I
            dare this.

DIONYSUS:

On you alone
falls the weight
            of this enterprise.
There are trials
which you must
            meet.
Come!
I am the guide

who will lead you to the mountains.

Another
shall carry you home.

PENTHEUS:

Yes—
my mother.

DIONYSUS:

All people
will see you.

PENTHEUS:

It is for that glory
I go.

DIONYSUS:

You will ride home . . .

PENTHEUS:

In luxury?

DIONYSUS:

In the arms
of your mother.

PENTHEUS:

You will make things
too soft for me.

DIONYSUS:

But such softness! 970

PENTHEUS:

Yet all this
is my due.

DIONYSUS:

You are a strange man;
you will suffer.
You will gain glory
that towers to heaven.
Agave and your sisters,
Cadmus' daughters,
                        make ready!

I lead this youth
into torment and danger. 975
Bromius and I shall win,
as events
            will soon show.

Exit Dionysus and Pentheus.

CHORUS:

Strophe

Hell-hounds of Lysa,
run to Cadmus' daughters in the mountains!
Sting them to madness
against this man in women's clothes,   980
this insane man
who spies on the Maenads!

His mother will see him among the rocks,
and as he stares
she will shout to the Maenads,
"Who spies on the daughter of Cadmus?   985
What must the mother
of such a creature be?
A monster?
A lioness?
A gorgon of Lydia?"   990

Let justice be seen,
sword in hand,
killing this   995
godless, lawless,
earth-born son
of Echion.

Antistrophe

Whoever blasphemes against you, Bacchus,
whoever rages against your mother's rites,
whoever thinks   1000
he can conquer the unconquerable
by bodily strength—
death will teach him wisdom.

But if humans accept, as they should,
all that the gods give,
they will live without pain.

Thinking brings no happiness,   1005
and I rejoice
doing what all people know
leads to a joyful life:
through lone days and nights
living pure and reverent,
avoiding all evil,
honouring the god.   1010

Let justice be seen,
sword in hand,
killing this
godless, lawless,   1015
earth-born son
of Echion.

Epode

Bull,
dragon,
raging lion,
join your hunters, Bromius!   1020
Laugh
and cast the net of death
over Pentheus!

Enter Messenger.

MESSENGER:

This house
was once
   the most prosperous
   in Greece,
the old man of Sidon's house.
One summer long ago
he, Cadmus, sowed the earth
   with dragon's teeth,
and men sprang up—   1025
his children.
Even I, a slave,
   am sad to see this . . .

CHORUS:

What has happened?
Have you news of Bacchae?

MESSENGER:

Pentheus,   1030
son of Echion,
   is dead.

CHORUS:

Bromius, King—
now all

can see

        your power!

MESSENGER:

What is that
you say?
Do you rejoice
in the fate
        of my master?

CHORUS:

Yes!
We cry *Evohe*
for we   1035
are no longer afraid
        to sing in this land.

MESSENGER:

Do you think Thebes
poor in people and spirit
that it cannot control you now?

CHORUS:

Dionysus—
Dionysus—
        not Thebes—
rules over me!

MESSENGER:

We might pardon everything   1040
but your exultation
over our ruin.

CHORUS:

Tell us—
tell us how
       this inventor of
           injustice
               died.

MESSENGER:

I followed my master and the stranger
through the Theban farmlands
across the streams of Asopus,
and up the bare crags of Cithaeron.   1045
At first we hid in a grassy hollow,
still and quiet
so we wouldn't be noticed.   1050
On the edge of this ravine
bounded by cliffs,
by tumbling water,
by thick shade-pines,
sat the Maenads,
their hands busy
gaily tying crowns of ivy on their sticks,
repairing their thyrsi.   1055

Others, like colts released from harness,
sang wild Bacchic songs to each other.
"Stranger,
from where we stand
I cannot view   1060
                these so-called Maenads
but if I climbed a hill
or perhaps a tall tree
                I could easily watch
                        their shameless conduct."

Then
I saw the stranger
                work a miracle.
He caught the top
of an enormous pine
and bent it,
bent it,
                down to the black earth.   1065
He bent it as a bow is bent
or as the rim of a wheel is fitted.
With his hands
the stranger bowed it to the earth
                as if it were a slender
                        stem.
No human could have done that.
Pentheus settled in the top boughs   1070
and slowly, carefully,
so that he would not fall
                or be tossed through the air,
the stranger released the pine.

To the height of heaven it rose,
bearing my master seated on its tip,
more seen by the Bacchae
than seeing them.   1075

As soon as Pentheus was visible to all,
the stranger vanished:
and from the sky
came a voice—
            that of Dionysus, I am sure—
crying:
"Maidens of mine,
I bring you him
            who has laughed at you   1080
                and my rites.
Punish him now."

Bright fire flashed between
heaven
            and earth.
The sky was silent.
The valley
            held its leaves still,
and you could hear   1085
no beasts
            crying.
But even the deaf heard Dionysus
and sprang up,
the pupils of their eyes
scanning the horizon.

Once more
he urged them on
till all the daughters
knew the commands of Bacchus
and, with the swiftness of wood pigeons,   1090
sprang down
across torrent and crag
                into the forest,
maddened
by the god's
                breath.

When they saw my master
hidden in the pine,
they climbed a towering rock
and hurled huge stones at him,
cast javelins of pine boughs
and tossed their thyrsi through the sky
                at wretched Pentheus.   1100
He was trapped
but seated
                beyond even their reach.

With branches
like oaken thunderbolts,
                they struck the tree,
tearing at the roots
with those levers,
but when their toil was ended   1105
the tree still stood.
Then Agave cried out,

"Maenads, come!
Circle this sapling,
hold it firmly—
we must seize this climbing beast
before he betrays to mankind
             the secrets of the god."
They tore the tree from the earth,   1110
and he who sat in the sky
fell wailing
into the soft dirt.
That his end had come
was clear
         to Pentheus.

Like a priestess at the sacrificial altar,
his mother
        began
           the slaughter.

Poor Agave.
He loosened the band from his hair   1115
that she might know him.
He touched her cheek, saying
"I am your son, Pentheus,
whom you bore in Echion's house—
have pity on me, mother, though I have sinned.
Do not kill your son."   1120
But she was mad,
with foam at her mouth,
and her eyes rolled wildly,
for she was possessed

by Bacchus
and could not think.   1125
She set her foot
against his ribs,
and, gripping his left arm
with the ease given
            by the god's strength,
tore off his shoulder.
Ino tore his flesh
on the other side.
Then Autonoe   1130
and the other Bacchantes
            fell on him.

One cry rose from Pentheus
while he had breath,
and blended
with their shouts
            of victory.

His arm, one foot with its sandal,
shreds of flesh from his sides
were tossed like balls
            from hand to bloody hand   1135
while his remains lay scattered
on sharp rocks
            and amongst
                    the forest leaves.
His battered head
was grasped by his mother,
rammed on the top of a thyrsus,

and carried through the wilds of Cithaeron
like the head
         of some mountain lion.
She left her Maenad sisters in the mountains
and comes,
         proud of her trophy,
            to these walls,
crying again and again,
         on the name of Bacchus.   1145
For her victory
all she will win
         shall be tears,
and therefore
I leave
before Agave
reaches this house.
For I believe   1150
that our most beautiful
         possessions
are sanity
and a love of the gods.
The wise are those
who use
      wisdom.

Exit Messenger.

CHORUS:

The dragon's child is dead.
Come cry *Evohe* to Bacchus!

Pentheus,
who in a woman's dress
briefly held
a bacchic staff
and died
because of its
glory—
Pentheus,
led to disaster,
                    is dead.
Cadmeian Bacchae,
you have made
a great hymn of victory,
            but its end will be weeping
                        and tears.
A beautiful victory,
to take with blood-covered hands
the life
            of your own
                    child.
I see her, running toward these halls—
Pentheus' mother, Agave,
her eyes wide with love
            for our merry-maker, Bacchus.

Enter Agave carrying Pentheus' head on her staff.

AGAVE:

Asian Bacchae!

CHORUS:

Why do you call me?

AGAVE:

We carry
fresh ivy from the mountain   1170
and bring
a blessed prey.

CHORUS:

Welcome, fellow reveler.

AGAVE:

I caught this young lion
without net or trap!   1175

CHORUS:

Who struck the first blow?

AGAVE:

That was my privilege.
My name will be praised
amid the revels.   1180

CHORUS:

Who struck the next blow?

AGAVE:

Cadmus . . .

CHORUS:

What of Cadmus?

AGAVE:

After I struck,
his daughters attacked this beast. Share with us
the prey
              we hunted.

CHORUS:

Share what, wretched woman?

AGAVE:

This animal
still young;   1185
there are tender hairs
around its jaw
under the crest of
its long mane.

CHORUS:

From its hair
one would think it
a wild beast.

AGAVE:

Bacchus, that skilled hunter,
roused the Maenads against it.   1190

CHORUS:

Our king is a hunter.

AGAVE:

Do you praise me?

CHORUS:

We praise . . .

AGAVE:

Soon the Cadmeians . . .

CHORUS:

And Pentheus, your son . . .   1195

AGAVE:

He too will praise his mother
for killing
this lion cub.

CHORUS:

A wild prey.

AGAVE:

Wildly taken.

CHORUS:

Do you rejoice?

AGAVE:

I rejoice greatly
that all may see I cornered this prey.

CHORUS:

Then,
poor woman,
show your victory prize,   1200
your treasure
which you have carried
        to this town.

AGAVE:

O beautiful, high-towered city of Thebes, O dwellers in this
land, behold this beast
that we,
        the daughters of Cadmus,
          caught,
not with javelins,   1205
not with hunting nets,
but with white hands,
with sharp fingers.

Why should the spear carriers and ace-wielders boast?
We took him with our bare hands!
We tore his flesh, ourselves.   1210

Where is my father?
Let him come here.
Where is Pentheus, my son?
Let him climb a ladder
            and nail to a beam of the house
                        the head of this lion.   1215

Enter Cadmus with servants carrying a litter on which lies
Pentheus' body.

CADMUS:

Servants,
follow me, carrying your pitiful load,
the body of Pentheus.
I found it after infinite toil,
torn to pieces
in the thick woods
                        on Cithaeron's side.   1220
As I walked with old Teiresias,
returning to Thebes from the mountain,
I was told of my daughter's deeds.
I went back   1225
and now I carry my grandson
killed
            by the Maenads.

There I saw her
who bore Actaeon to Aristaeus, Autonoe,
        and Ino,
those wretched women,
        still stung mad
           among the rocks.
But someone told me that Agave   1230
had come here,
        dancing wildly.
And that is true.
I see her
        and the sight brings me
           no joy.

AGAVE:

Father,
you may boast
that of all mortals
you have the noblest daughter!
I left the looms and combs for greater things,   1235
to hunt wild beasts with my hands.
See,
I bring in my arms
        a great prize
           to hang against the house.

Father, take it   1240
in your hands
and pride
yourself in my prey.

Invite your friends to celebrate this triumph.
How fortunate you are
        that we
             have won this victory!

CADMUS:

I wish no man sadness infinite as mine—
this murder done by those hands—   1245
this young victim sacrificed for the gods—
this invitation to a feast of mourning.
Woe for your misfortune, then for mine!
God has dealt justly with us.
But Dionysus, King,   1250
you are cruel to destroy your own family.

AGAVE:

How old age makes men discontented and sullen.
I hope my son
will have his mother's luck
when he and the Theban youths
chase the wild beasts.   1255
That one—
he seems fit to fight
        alone against the gods.

Father, you must warn him
        against that.

Now, who will call him here
to see me
                    and my luck?

CADMUS:

O, when you understand what evil you have done,
your grief . . .   1260
                    You are not lucky,
                    but if you continue dreaming
you may
                    escape misery.

AGAVE:

What is wrong here?

CADMUS:

First, look up to bright heaven.

AGAVE:

There,
but why?   1265

CADMUS:

Does the sky
still look the same?
Or has it changed?

AGAVE:

I do not understand! 1270
Somehow
    a change
        has come
            on my mind,
a freeing . . .

CADMUS:

Can you answer my questions reasonably?

AGAVE:

Father,
I have forgotten
        everything you were saying.

CADMUS:

To whose house were you brought amid marriage songs?

AGAVE:

To the house of one of those men
        who sprang from dragon's teeth.
To Echion you gave me. 1275

CADMUS:

What child did you bear your husband in these halls?

AGAVE:

Pentheus, his father's true son.

CADMUS:

And whose head is it
you hold in your arms?

AGAVE:

A lion's—or so the huntress told me.

CADMUS:

Look at it carefully.
It is easy to look.

AGAVE:

What prize   1280
have I
               in my hands?

CADMUS:

Look at it.
Know the truth.

AGAVE:

I see
disaster.

CADMUS:

It is not like a lion's head now?

AGAVE:

It is Pentheus' head I hold.

CADMUS:

I mourned him   1285
long before you knew.

AGAVE:

Who killed him?
Why is he in my hands?

CADMUS:

You and your sisters murdered him.

AGAVE:

Where?

CADMUS:

Where Actaeon was torn to pieces
by his hound.

AGAVE:

Why did he go to Cithaeron?

CADMUS:

He went to mock the god
and your Bacchic rites.

AGAVE:

Why did we go there?

CADMUS:

The whole city was driven mad by Bacchus.   1295

AGAVE:

I understand now—
we have been destroyed by Dionysus.

CADMUS:

You insulted him.
You did not believe
he
          was a god.

AGAVE:

Father,
where is the body
          of my son?

CADMUS:

Here.
Full of sorrow,

104

I gathered it
and brought it.

AGAVE:

Was the flesh   1300
laid out properly?

CADMUS:

No, it is still in pieces
as I found it among the forest leaves.

AGAVE:

Why should Pentheus pay for my folly?

CADMUS:

Like you
he did not worship
            this god
who has bound us all
in our destruction.
My house and I will perish
for I have no sons of my own,   1305
and this child of yours, poor Agave,
killed amid such evil and shame—
he was the hope of my family;
he held my house together.

Son of my daughter,
the whole city was in awe of you.   1310

No one dared to insult an old man
once he had seen your face, for justly you would have punished
such a fool.
Now I shall be driven away in dishonour,
exiled from my house—
I, great Cadmus,
who sowed the seed
of the Theban race
and reaped a fine harvest.   1315

Beloved grandson,
though you are dead,
my child, still
you shall be dearest of all men to me.
Though you shall never touch my cheek again

and ask . . . and ask who wrongs me,
ask, "Who has slighted the old man now?   1320
Who has upset you
and pained your heart?
Tell me, grandfather,

for I would punish such fools."
Now indeed am I a pitiful man,
you a pitiful mother,
and pitiful all our family.
If anyone, anywhere, denies the gods,   1325
seeing this death
let him believe in them.

CHORUS:

I grieve for you, Cadmus.
But, whatever the pain to your family,
Pentheus received justice.

AGAVE:

Father,
see
     how,
in a moment,
        my life has been changed
from a blessed one
to one of despair.
Let me lay this body out for burial
though our last farewells
do the dead no good.

CADMUS:

Poor Agave,
now, learn the horror
      of your work in the mountains.
And taking all care you can
prepare Pentheus for burial—
his limbs like the land
      ploughed, furrowed and spattered
        with blood.
Let all mortals
Learn how Zeus reveals

he is the father
> of Dionysus, the god.

AGAVE:

How gently must I hold him
to my heart.
How can I sing a dirge
when I have only broken flesh
> to praise?
Let us place his flesh together
that I might embrace him.
Let us lay his head straight;
let me cover his head with my veil;
let us place his limbs together;
let us make him,
as far as we can,
like that strong youth he was.

If he had lived,
I believe he might have become
a man filled with joy.

Dionysus appears in splendor on a level above the palace.

DIONYSUS:

Bacchae,
we have our victory.

CHORUS:

Come cry *Evohe*
to Bacchus!

DIONYSUS:

People of Thebes, who rejected my gifts
and denied
 my divine birth,
Agave, listen.

Pentheus, whose sad corpse you hold in your arms,
mocked
me.
Pentheus made war against your wild dancers
on the mountain.
Pentheus tried to bind me with chains
and mocked me.
Therefore, he was murdered
by those who most loved him.
This was his punishment,
and I will not hide the truth from you—
Thebans
 must suffer again.

You shall surrender this land to strangers
and be marched to many far cities
wearing the yoke of slavery,
tormented
because
you disowned
 Dionysus.
Agave, you and your sisters

must leave this city now
to pay for your guilt.
You shall never see your country again.
Murderers must not sleep
in their victims' graves.

And this man,
Cadmus—
he, above all,
will live in misery.
You and your wife, Harmonia, daughter of Aries,   1330
shall be changed to wild serpents
and drive a chariot
leading a barbarian host.   1335
Many cities
will be ravaged
           in your numberless campaigns,
even the oracle shrine of Apollo.

You shall have a long and bitter journey,
but in the end
you and Harmonia
shall rescue Aries from peril,

and I will take you
alive
           to Elysium.

I, Dionysus,   1340
son of Zeus,
           no son of mortal father,
              promise this.

But if you had shown more wisdom,
I would have been your ally now.

CADMUS:

Dionysus,
we beg forgiveness—
            we know we have sinned.

DIONYSUS:

It is too late
to acknowledge me.
There was a time   1345
when you needed me,
            and you did not admit I exist.

CADMUS:

We know that—
but you are too harsh.

DIONYSUS:

You insulted a god.

CADMUS:

Gods should not have human tempers.

DIONYSUS:

Long ago, my father Zeus
agreed that they could.

AGAVE:

Then   1350
we must go
                    into exile.

DIONYSUS:

Why do you delay?
There is nothing more to do.
Exit Dionysus.

CADMUS:

Child,
this is our end—
yours, your wretched sisters', and mine.
By this decree
in my old age,
                    I shall reach a foreign land
                              and settle there.   1355
In the form of dragons,
Harmonia and I
must command troops of barbarian spear men
                    against our own Greek altars and graves.
I will never rest,   1360
never die and find peace,
for I shall sail alive
down the plunging
                    Acheron.

AGAVE:

Father,
you shall be taken from me
                    and exiled.

CADMUS:

Why embrace me, child,
like a young swan
protecting a white, helpless, old one?   1365

AGAVE:

My home, city of my father, farewell.
I forsake you
in misery,
in exile fleeing   1370
my bridal chamber.

CADMUS:

Farewell, my child.

AGAVE:

I shall mourn for you, father.

CADMUS:

And I for you,
and for all your sisters.

AGAVE:

Dionysus, the King,
has cursed you and your house terribly. 1375

DIONYSUS:

Off stage.

I was insulted.
My name was dishonoured in Thebes.

AGAVE:

Farewell, my father.

CADMUS:

Farewell, my unhappy daughter.
You will have no joy. 1380

Exit Cadmus.

AGAVE:

My friends,
take me to my sisters,
            my fellow exiles,
that we may find our doom
and go where blood-stained Cithaeron 1385
shall not look down on me,
where no thyrsus shall honour the dead.
Let this be the care
of other Bacchae.

Exit Agave.

CHORUS:

The shapes of god shift
through many forms,
and lives are changed
more than we
                    could dream.
What we thought would happen
did not,
but we
have seen the god reveal
the true order
                    of the world.

Exit Chorus.